The
Music
Box
Roberto Jime
The
Music
Box

The Music Box

Roberto Jimenez

Published by Roberto Jimenez, 2024.

THE MUSIC BOX

First edition. September 13, 2024.

Copyright © 2024 Roberto Jimenez.

ISBN: 979-8986616742

Written by Roberto Jimenez.

Table of Contents

Foreword

On Christmas Eve, Lucia has an unpleasant encounter with a repairman at a hotel. Although this chance meeting seems insignificant at first, their paths cross again at a nearby hospital, leading to a profound shift in Lucia's thoughts and actions. In the following hours, she embarks on a determined search for an object—a music box. For the first time, she is driven to do something selfless for a stranger, and nothing can dissuade her from her plan.

In this intense and touching story, Roberto Jimenez crafts a narrative grounded in hope, sensitivity, compassion, and perseverance. Lucia's journey is sure to deeply affect readers, offering a powerful reflection on the impact of kindness in our lives.

Edelmis Anoceto Vega

To my children, "Be not careless in deeds, nor confused in words, nor rambling in thought."

– Marcus Aurelius

Preface

Dear Reader,

I invite you to step into the world of "The Music Box," a story that holds a special place in my heart. This tale first took shape during my university years, a time when I observed how often we, as young adults, drift through life, unaware of how our actions touch the lives of others. I hope that through the journey of Victor and Lucia, you, too, will find a moment to pause and reflect.

In the midst of a bustling city, blanketed by the serene hush of falling snow, a father carries a gift of immeasurable value —a music box wrapped in pink and white, destined for his ailing daughter. This box is more than a mere object; it is a vessel of hope, a promise of love, and a fragment of joy amidst the shadows of illness.

As you turn the pages, you will meet Victor, a weary maintenance man, and Lucia, a woman struggling with her own moral compass. Their lives intersect in a moment of chance, setting the stage for a story of redemption and realization. It is through their eyes that I hope to convey a message close to my heart: the profound impact our most minor acts can have.

We live in a world that often moves too quickly, blinding us to the needs of those around us. Through this narrative, I wish to awaken a sense of compassion and awareness in each of you.

Let this story be a reminder to pause, to see, and to care, for it is in these genuine connections that we find the true essence of our humanity.

Thank you for joining me on this journey. May "The Music Box" inspire you to cherish each moment and to recognize the ripples of your actions in the lives of others.

With heartfelt gratitude,

Roberto Jimenez

♫CHAPTER ONE♫

The Elevator

Victor could hardly contain his exhaustion as he stood inside the elevator. He closely watched the digital readout displaying the ascending floor numbers; each seemed to drag on, reminding him of the long twelve-hour shift he had endured. Fatigue weighed heavily on his shoulders, and he longed for this to be the final repair on his list for the night, yearning for some well-deserved rest.

He glanced out the elevator window, taking in the city illuminated with festive lights, a glimpse from each passing-by floor at a time. Red and green displays shaped like Christmas trees adorned one building, while another showcased 'Season's Greetings' in gold lettering. Snow had started falling a few hours ago, and now a steady stream of flakes cascaded from the sky.

The elevator stopped and emitted a soft ding as the doors slid open, revealing the expansive view from the thirty-sixth floor. Stepping onto the floor of the hotel's most expensive suites, Victor smoothed down his work uniform, ensuring his nametag and the company logo were visible, and walked down the hallway to the end. Knocking softly on the door, he called out, "Maintenance."

The door opened, revealing a well-dressed older woman. "Oh, thank goodness you're here! It's right this way."

Her attire consisted of a pristine white suit adorned with a delicate sprig of holly affixed to the lapel. The distinct clicking of her high heels on the marble floor resonated through the hallway as she guided Victor toward the luxurious ensuite bathroom.

"The sink has been leaking for about an hour now, and I'm unsure how to stop it."

Victor smiled, setting his toolbox on the edge of the sink. "No problem, ma'am. I'll have this fixed in no time at all."

"Thank you so much! I have to be at a party in about an hour, and I didn't want to leave it like this. And even though I hated calling the front desk, I didn't want to return to a flooded bathroom."

"You did the right thing, ma'am. I'll clean up all this excess water and have everything back to normal."

The woman nodded and walked back into the living room while Victor pulled out his wrench and got to work. As he did, he could hear the soft strains of Christmas music playing from the living room, mingling with the muted sounds of the city outside. Victor knelt by the sink, water pooling across the floor from a steady leak. After inspecting the pipes, he identified the issue—a faulty valve that wasn't sealing properly. With a few quick twists of his wrench, he replaced the valve, tightened the surrounding bolts, and tested the flow. The water stopped almost immediately. Working swiftly, he mopped up the excess water with an old towel, ensuring the floor was dry. Satisfied with the repair, Victor grabbed his toolbox and stepped out of the bathroom. The woman was sitting on the sofa, sipping a cocktail, her eyes meeting his as she waited.

"All finished here," Victor told her.

"It shouldn't give you any more problems. There was a faulty valve, but I've replaced it and made sure everything else is in working order."

"Thank you so much, and I'm so sorry to bother you this late on Christmas Eve. I had no idea they would have maintenance working tonight."

Victor smiled. "Of course, ma'am. Happy to help."

"Have you been busy today?" she asked, crossing the room to walk him to the door.

"A bit less than usual, but it's been steady," he replied.

"I can't imagine the hotel still has many guests here this evening," she remarked. "I can't wait to head out in the morning to visit my daughter's lovely home in the suburbs."

"Yes, ma'am, I believe many guests have left for the holidays already, but there are still a few here. Hopefully, the snow lets up overnight, so you have a safer drive in the morning."

The woman smiled warmly. "Thank you so much, Mr. ...?"

"You can call me Victor, ma'am. And if you need anything else, don't hesitate to call the front desk."

"Thank you, Victor." She grabbed her purse from a table next to the door, pulled out a bill, and offered it to him. "Let me give you a little something. It's the least I can do."

Victor smiled and shook his head. "I'm just doing my job, ma'am. No gratuity necessary."

She nodded and put the money back in her purse. "Well then, Merry Christmas to you, Victor."

He opened the door and stepped out into the hallway. "And a Merry Christmas to you too, ma'am."

Closing the door behind him, Victor walked back down the hall to the elevator, not surprised to find the elevator car still waiting for him. The hotel, usually bustling with guests, was unusually quiet tonight. He took out a key for the subfloors, inserted it, and pressed the button for B2, the basement where the maintenance office was located. He leaned back against the wall to observe the city lights whisk by as the elevator descended, the darkness of the night sky making it feel much later than it was.

The elevator doors opened, and Victor stepped into a service hallway. Walking a few doors down, he entered his workshop and set his toolbox on a nearby bench. Sitting at his desk, he added the service ticket from the last room to the stack of 'completed work orders' for that day. The incoming maintenance man was on call for the night, so Victor didn't see the need to tidy things up much; he'd be back soon enough.

Finally letting out a long yawn, he got up, walked to the locker room, undressed, and took a quick, hot shower to wash away the day's dirt and grime. Feeling renewed from the shower and after wiping away the steam from the mirror, he combed back his slick black hair, now tinged with a few gray spots. He looked reasonably young for being in his early forties, but a few wrinkles reminded him he was no longer twenty-five.

He walked to his locker, pulled out a fresh set of clothes, and quickly put them on, adding boots and a thick coat at the end in preparation for the cold walk that awaited him to get to his car. It would be a long trip across town tonight, especially if the city hadn't cleared the roads. He doubted any snowplow trucks had made their way into the city on Christmas Eve; they were probably home with their families, just like everyone else.

Grabbing his hat and scarf, he pulled them on and folded his work uniform neatly into his knapsack to take home for laundry later. The last thing he grabbed was a square-shaped package wrapped in brown paper. He reached to the top shelf of the locker and pulled it down, smiling at the box as he closed the locker door.

Turning off the lights and locking up his workshop, he walked back down the hall, carrying the package. Pressing the elevator button, he waited a few minutes for the car to return. Although not very big, the box was heavy. He opened the lid and peered inside, smiling at the contents. It had taken him weeks to find the right one, and now that the moment had finally come, he could hardly wait to deliver it.

The elevator dinged, the doors split open, and Victor stepped inside, hitting the button for the lobby. Although he liked his job well enough, he was happy to leave the hotel for the night. As the elevator rose, he thought about the snow falling gently outside and the twinkling lights decorating the city. Although the streets would be quiet, the journey would still take longer on a snowy night, but the anticipation of giving the gift kept him warm. When the elevator stopped, Victor felt ready to take on the icy roads, and happy to finally get to see her again.

♫CHAPTER TWO♫

An Untimely Collision

"**M**ore champagne, my sweet?"

Lucia turned her head to Marco, her eyes glinting with a mischievous light as her fingers curled elegantly around the slender stem of the glass. "Do I ever say no to more champagne?"

Their laughter, light and unrestrained, filled the intimate space of the limousine. Marco tilted the bottle, pouring a generous stream of effervescent liquid into her glass, a few drops cascading over the edge and splashing onto her red satin dress.

"My apologies, love. We must've encountered a bump in the road."

Lucia took a generous sip and then set the glass down on the small bar beside her. "There aren't any potholes on these roads! We're in the finest part of the city!"

Marco's gaze shifted to the passing scenery outside the window. "Ah, you're right. It seems we're arriving sooner than expected. We should savor our moments here."

Her lips curved into a sly smile, feigned innocence dancing in her eyes. "Why, Marco, whatever could you mean?"

His hand found its way to her knee, fingers tracing a path beneath the hem of her dress. "I think you always know what I have in mind, Gorgeous." Marco felt enchanted by her voice, which flowed like a soft melody through the air. He was drawn in, unable to resist the urge to kiss her with passion.

The holiday reception they had just left had been dull compared to Lucia's usual escapades, but the open bar had provided ample entertainment. She had indulged more than usual, but it was a party, after all. For his part, Marco appeared to delight in her intoxication, his fondness increasing with each drink she had.

Lucia pushed him back into his seat, straddling his lap. As she glanced out the window, her eyes widened in delight. "Marco! It's snowing! You didn't tell me it was snowing!"

"It was snowing when we got into the limo earlier, dear," he said, his laughter a deep, resonant sound.

With a gleeful laugh, she reached up and pressed the button to open the sunroof.

"Lucia! What are you doing? You'll freeze!"

Ignoring his protest, she kicked off her heels and stood precariously on the seat, lifting herself through the opening. Snowflakes whipped past, stinging her bare arms and chest with their icy touch, but she barely noticed. She spread her arms wide, leaning back and closing her eyes, a smile of pure joy on her lips as the snow dampened her hair and dress. Marco's hands found her waist, pulling her back down and closing the sunroof.

"You're mad, you know that?" he said, brushing snow from her hair.

"Isn't that what you wanted?" she teased, her smile never fading. "A wild, crazy girl who does outlandish things?"

He stroked her cheek tenderly, his lips brushing against hers. "I suppose you're right."

"Mmmhmm." She drained the rest of her champagne, let the glass slip from her fingers to the carpeted floor, and then wrapped her arms around his neck. "Now, let's see how far we can go before this ride ends."

Several minutes later, the limousine glided to a stop before the entrance of the grand hotel Marco had reserved for the night. Lucia, her laughter a soft melody, hastily attempted to rearrange the neckline of her dress before one of the doormen approached and opened the limo's door.

"Good evening, Mr. –"

"Thank you, but we'll need one more minute." Marco intercepted, shutting the door in the doorman's face as Lucia slipped her heels back on her feet.

"The only man who's going to see you looking delightfully disheveled tonight is me," Marco murmured, his voice a mix of possessiveness and adoration.

Lucia, now composed, leaned over him and seductively whispered, "I'm fine now, baby," as she proceeded to open the door herself.

"Sorry about that," she called out to the doorman with a now playful smile.

Marco stepped out of the limo, extending both hands to help her. She stumbled slightly as her feet met the pavement.

"Can you walk?" he asked, his grin wide.

"As long as you keep your hands on me," she replied, giggling softly, her voice a symphony of joy.

They carelessly entered the hotel, its opulent interior a testament to luxury. Lucia glanced around, her eyes wide with wonder at the large chandelier, the velvet couches, and the intricate Persian rug on the parquet floor. This was one of the finest hotels around, and she reveled in the thought of staying here, courtesy of Marco's generosity.

"Honey, you ready?" Marco twirled her around, holding up their room key.

"Mmm." She smiled and kissed him unabashedly, in full view of the two young women at the front desk. The clerks exchanged awkward glances as Marco and Lucia obnoxiously moved toward the bank of elevators.

"I got us one of the suites on the top floor," Marco whispered between kisses. "They're supposed to be the best in the city."

Lucia's smile widened. "I'm going to show you the best time in that suite tonight," she said between kisses.

Marco chuckled and said, "You better. That room cost me a pretty penny."

Marco glanced around impatiently. "Don't they have more than one of these things working?" he grumbled, pulling Lucia closer.

"Oh-oh, do you want to d-dance?" she slurred slightly, taking his hand and twirling herself around towards the elevator doors.

Unbeknownst to her, the elevator had just arrived, and its doors quickly opened. Victor had begun making his way out of the elevator as Lucia spun right onto him, both stumbling back from the collision.

"Watch it!" she shrieked, falling into Marco's waiting arms and feeling terribly embarrassed.

The collision caused Victor to trip backward, sending the bundle he held flying. They watched the package finally hit the floor, making a resounding clunk sound. Its contents spilled out and shattered into countless pieces.

Lucia recoiled, ensuring none of the debris touched her. Victor composed himself and made a delayed and futile effort to catch the now-broken package.

"You idiot!" she screamed. "Don't you ever watch where you're going? How was I supposed to know you'd come barreling out of the elevator like that? It's not my fault you can't look before you go somewhere!"

Trying to soothe her, Marco wrapped his arms around Lucia and guided her towards the elevator. "Come on now, baby, don't worry. It was just a mistake–"

"A very avoidable mistake!" she retorted as Victor knelt to gather the broken pieces. "Maybe you should get glasses because you obviously can't see very well."

Marco chuckled. "You sure are a firecracker when you drink, aren't you? Come on, let's go up to the room. I ordered some champagne, and it should be waiting for us by the time we get upstairs."

"Not until he apologizes! I'm in very high heels, Marco. He could've knocked me over and seriously hurt me!" Lucia fumed, crossing her arms and glaring at Victor, who continued to ignore her. Finally, she sighed, exasperated, and melted back into Marco's embrace as he pushed one of the top floor buttons.

"This is boring. Let's get out of here."

As the doors closed, Victor looked at the shattered remnants of his package, feeling a wave of helplessness wash over him. He carefully gathered the broken pieces into the torn paper, wrapping it again with care. Holding it close, Victor exited the hotel and walked to his car parked on a side street, his steps cautious on the icy sidewalk. Once inside, he laid the damaged package gently on the passenger seat, even though it no longer mattered how carefully he handled it now; what it contained was irrevocably lost.

♫CHAPTER THREE♫

A Fragmented Promise

As he inserted the key into the ignition and awaited the car's sputtering start, Victor's mind raced with the gravity of his predicament. It was Christmas Eve, and the prospect of replacing the package now seemed an exercise in futility. Yet, a flicker of hope pierced his despair. His gaze settled on a luminous, red billboard ahead, proclaiming the extended hours of a popular department store, a beacon for last-minute shoppers.

Determination mingled with uncertainty in Victor's heart. Could this store hold the replacement he so desperately sought? He had to try. Maneuvering his car cautiously through the snow-laden streets, he advanced towards the store, perched atop a formidable hill. The treacherous conditions threatened to derail his mission, but his resolve steered him forward.

As he neared the store, its inviting lights pierced the wintery gloom, guiding him to a nearby parking spot. The deserted street, blanketed in snow, seemed to echo his isolation. Bracing against the biting cold, he stepped out, securing his coat tightly against the chill. The snow fell heavier now, the world around him would be frozen solid by morning, and he knew time was his enemy; he couldn't afford to linger.

Entering the store, a rush of warm air and bright lights greeted him. Shedding his damp hat and gloves, he blinked away the brightness, acclimating to the bustling interior. Multiple floors lay before him, each a labyrinth of potential and frustration. Methodically, he scoured each level, consulting with sales associates, but each encounter ended in disappointment.

Leaving empty-handed, a wave of discouragement washed over him. Yet, across the street, another store's lights flickered invitingly. He pressed on, undeterred, committed to his quest. The snow crunched beneath his boots as he crossed the street, glancing back at his car, the windshield already cloaked in a fresh layer of snowflakes.

The second store proved a brief, futile detour. Its nearly barren shelves offered no solace. Emerging into the frigid night, he cleared the snow from his windshield, his breath misting in the cold air. Inside the car, a joyful Christmas carol filled the silence. He switched off the radio, the cheerfulness starkly contrasting his somber mood.

Victor drove for hours, tirelessly seeking salvation in every open store. Each time, he was met with sympathetic smiles and well-wishes of 'Merry Christmas,' empty words that did little to lift his spirits. The city's festive lights and decorations blurred into a backdrop during his relentless pursuit, a quest that seemed increasingly hopeless.

With each unsuccessful stop, the weight of this failure grew. Once back in the car, he felt the stifling heat of the interior as he unbuttoned his jacket and contemplated his next move. Should he venture to the next town? Would there be any stores still open at this late hour?

As he pulled into the highway's turning lane, a blinking sign warned of hazardous conditions ahead; "Black Ice," it cautioned. It would have been irresponsible to continue. He decided to turn onto a side street and find an empty spot to park. For what it felt like a long while, he sat in silence.

Victor grappled with the disappointing search as best he could. At that moment, he closed his eyes and wished he had taken the stairs instead of the elevator that evening. He waited a few moments longer before heading to his final destination for the evening, replaying each decision he made in his mind, scanning for hope. However, reality was unyielding; he had to face the fact that he would arrive empty-handed.

A streetlight nearby cast a soft glow on the falling snow, each flake having a life of its own. The allure of snowball fights, building snowmen, and sledding held no joy in this moment, buried beneath his numbness. He watched his breath cloud the air, turned the car back on, and cranked up the heat.

"No point in staying here and freezing," he muttered as he drove back onto the street, heading for the other side of the city.

A DJ's monotone voice on the radio, a stark contrast to the festive songs of the season, provided a bleak comfort. He had hoped to make this Christmas memorable, but the incident at the hotel and the now-shattered package had extinguished that wish. Now, he had nothing worthwhile to give, and the promise he had made lay in fragments, much like the broken box.

♫CHAPTER FOUR♫

Poignant Juxtaposition

The elevator doors chimed softly as they opened, and Lucia emerged, her delicate fingers clutching the hem of her long dress to keep it from tangling beneath her feet. She swayed unsteadily, eventually finding support against the cold, unfeeling wall. A cascade of giggles escaped her lips as Marco approached, his strong hands encircling her waist to steady her.

"It doesn't take much to get you drunk," Marco remarked, his voice a low, rumbling chuckle.

Lucia glanced up at him, her expression feigning offense. "Drunk? I'm not drunk! Just... a little tipsy." She meandered down the dimly lit hallway, her movements erratic yet retaining an odd grace, one hand trailing along the wall for support.

Marco followed her, his steps measured and assured. He caught up to her, his arm once more around her waist. "The room is this way, Gorgeous."

"Mmm..." She looked up at him, her eyes gleaming with mischief, and pulled his head down to hers, their lips meeting in a fervent kiss.

"Okay, okay, let's get to the room first. We don't need to give anyone a show out here in the hallway." Marco guided her to the last room on the right, producing a key card. With a soft click, the door swung open, and Lucia waltzed inside, immediately kicking off her heels as she made her way to the bar in the spacious living room.

"Ah, the champagne you ordered." Lucia seized the bottle, struggling with the cork. Marco stepped behind her, gently taking the bottle from her hands and placing it back on the bar.

"The champagne can wait," he murmured, his arms wrapping around her. "First, I have to have you."

Lucia smiled, her arms entwining around his neck. "Then have me."

Marco led her into the bedroom, his fingers deftly lowering the zipper of her dress. Lucia stepped out of the stained, crimson gown, revealing the expensive lingerie he had gifted her. She reclined on the soft bed, her vision spinning, and embraced the sensation. Brusquely, he climbed on top of her, his attentions swift and fervent, a fleeting moment of passion.

When he finished, Marco rolled off Lucia and stretched out on the other side of the bed. Lucia stared up at the ceiling, the spinning room now still. A headache began to throb at her temples, likely from the champagne.

Marco stood, opening the balcony doors to let in the crisp night air, stepping outside to light a cigarette. Lucia shivered as the cold breeze filtered in, drawing the covers tighter over her bare skin. "Shut the door," she implored as a few delicate snowflakes wafted into the room.

Marco, smirking, closed the door partially, allowing the chill to linger. Lucia sighed, her mind drifting back to the evening's events. It had been an affair of sophistication and elegance, a striking departure from the dim, noisy dive bars and dance clubs she usually frequented. Marco had insisted on attending the grand gala, sparing no expense—hotel room, her dress, everything meticulously arranged.

Yet, despite all Marco provided, Lucia felt a gnawing dissatisfaction, especially after their fleeting encounter. His generosity lacked an essence of genuineness, and she was slowly realizing her own indifference towards him. Their time together, while amusing, felt devoid of substance and meaning.

Marco returned, completely shutting the door this time. With a mischievous grin, he approached the bed and playfully tugged the covers off her.

"I was cold!" Lucia protested, giggling as she attempted to reclaim the covers.

"You should never cover up, babe," Marco teased, his grin widening. "You're too sexy for that."

He climbed onto the mattress, advancing toward her with the grace of a predator closing in on its prey. Lucia squealed as he grasped her ankle, pulling her towards him for another round. She forced a smile, closed her eyes, and kissed him, hoping this encounter would surpass the brevity of the last.

"That was... great, actually," Lucia said a short while later, breathless. Though emotional depth eluded them, their physical chemistry occasionally hit the mark.

Marco turned, a smug smile playing on his lips, planting a quick kiss on her mouth. "I'm going to take a shower."

As he disappeared into the bathroom, Lucia stood, retrieving a robe from the wardrobe. She walked over to the bar, bypassing the champagne for a large glass bottle of water from the minibar fridge. Unscrewing the top, she filled a glass to the brim, drank it in one gulp, and then filled it again. As she downed the second glass, she felt her headache recede.

Returning to the bedroom, she picked up her gown and hung it up, frowning at the wrinkles marring the red satin. She'd need to have it professionally steamed, though she wondered where she might wear it again. Red satin was not really her style, except perhaps during the holidays.

Sitting on the edge of the bed, Lucia surveyed the room, a familiar wave of dissatisfaction washing over her. Marco's suit jacket lay crumpled at her feet. She bent to pick it up, intending to place it neatly on the bed. As she did, a small object slipped from one of the pockets, landing with a soft thud on the carpet. It caught the light, drawing her attention.

She reached down and picked up the object, turning it over in her palm. It was a gold band, unmistakably a wedding ring. The revelation struck her with an unexpected force. Marco had never mentioned a previous marriage. Or that he was currently married.

Lucia returned the ring to his jacket pocket and draped the garment over a nearby chair. She rationalized that Marco's personal life was none of her business. Their relationship was meant to be casual, a source of fleeting enjoyment. They had been seeing each other for just two months, and even then, it was only a couple of nights a week. She convinced herself she was content with this arrangement.

She finished her glass of water and set it on the nightstand before sinking back onto the bed. Reaching for the remote, she turned on the TV. A classic Christmas movie flickered on the screen, one she vaguely remembered from her childhood.

She recalled it being Christmas Eve, though the realization brought her little comfort. Her parents were away on a cruise, and she had no plans for the next day. She resigned to staying home, nursing the hangover she was sure to have, and perhaps ordering Chinese food. If Marco was indeed married, he would likely spend the holiday with his wife. Did he have children? The thought troubled her briefly before she dismissed it. His life outside their time together was not her concern.

Yet, an uneasy feeling gnawed at her. Was it the recognition of another meaningless relationship destined to go nowhere? Or the unsettling realization that she was now 'the other woman'?

Lucia had never played that role before. She wondered if Marco's wife knew and accepted the situation, perhaps turning a blind eye to his infidelities. But if that were the case, why would Marco hide it? It dawned on her that his wife was likely oblivious to his deceit.

The whole scenario left a bitter taste in her mouth. She wished she had never picked up his jacket or discovered the ring. Returning to the bar, she drained the remaining water from the bottle, the effects of the champagne fading. She grabbed a few wrapped chocolates and retreated to the bedroom, lying down and forcing herself to accept her part in an extramarital affair. She resolved not to dwell on it any further.

Popping a chocolate candy into her mouth, she ignored the feeling of unease in her stomach and settled to watch the remainder of the Christmas movie. The sound of the shower ceased, and she heard Marco moving around in the bathroom. She wondered if he would want to go for another round once he emerged. She wasn't sure if she felt up to it, but she could probably persuade herself.

As she let out a long yawn, the familiar ring of her phone interrupted her thoughts. Springing from the bed, she hurried into the next room, her eyes scanning for her misplaced purse. She found it lying next to the bar, discarded in her eagerness to open the bottle of champagne earlier. Retrieving her phone, she was puzzled to see an unfamiliar number. Who could be calling at this late hour?

She hit the answer button and held the phone to her ear.

"Hello?"

"Is this Lucia Romano?" a serious voice inquired.

"Yes, this is she."

"Miss Romano, this is Officer Peterson. I'm calling concerning Liam Romano."

"Liam? What has my brother done now?" She had known it was a mistake when their parents left him home alone for a week while they went on vacation. Sixteen might be old enough in years, but not necessarily in responsibility. She'd visited her parents' house earlier that day, and Liam promised her he wouldn't get into trouble. Obviously, that promise was broken.

"Your brother was involved in an accident and has been transferred to Children's Hospital. We tried reaching your parents, but they were unavailable. You were the next contact."

Lucia nearly dropped the phone. "Oh, my goodness. Is he alright? What happened? What happened to my brother?" Her voice rose in panic.

"My apologies, but I'm not allowed to discuss his injuries over the phone. You should come to the hospital as soon as you can."

Her breathing became shallow and rapid as the urgency of the situation gripped her. "I'll be right there," she replied.

After hanging up, Lucia rushed to the closet, hastily pulling her dress from the hanger and stepping into it, fumbling with the zipper at the back. She didn't have time to return to her apartment and change; she would have to go as she was. At that moment, Marco emerged from the bathroom, towel-drying his hair. His expression turned to a frown when he saw her dressed.

"You're not leaving me, are you?"

"Well, sort of." She reached for her coat, her movements hurried. "It's my brother. He's been in an accident, and I have to go to the hospital now."

Marco's eyes widened, a mix of shock and concern shadowing his face. "Oh, I'm so sorry." He watched her dart back and forth between the bedroom and the living room, gathering her belongings in a frantic dance of worry. "Can I take you there?"

She paused, turning to face him, a mixture of urgency and frustration in her eyes. "How? You didn't drive us here, remember?"

Marco nodded, the realization settling in. "Right, but I can call a car for us."

She nodded, her eyes flickering with a brief moment of relief. "That would be easier than trying to find a taxi this late at night," she said, slipping her phone into her coat pocket with trembling hands.

"Alright. Let me get dressed, and I'll be right out. Just go in the other room and try to relax."

She gave him a look of disbelief. "Relax? My brother's lying in the hospital, and my parents aren't around. I have no idea what's happened to him or how bad it really is. How am I supposed to relax in a moment like this?"

"Right. Sorry." Marco offered her a sympathetic smile, his anxiety poorly masked as he grabbed his pants from the floor. She entered the other room, her eyes catching the glint of the unopened champagne bottle. For a fleeting moment, she wished she had indulged. Perhaps a drink would have steadied her nerves and quelled the storm of worry within her.

Her mind raced, burdened with thoughts of her brother. Why did their parents have to leave him alone? Why couldn't they have taken him with them? Now, the responsibility fell on her shoulders; for all she knew, he might be teetering on the edge between life and death.

♫CHAPTER FIVE♫

Encounters

After Marco dressed and called for a car to come and pick them up, they headed down the hall to the elevator. Lucia's mind wandered back to the moment earlier in the evening when the man from the elevator had bumped into her, dropping his package. The floor had been littered with pink and white shards, glistening like shattered dreams. He should have been more careful, but she knew she shared the blame deep down. Not that she'd ever admit it aloud.

Now was not the moment to dwell on the man and his broken package. Her thoughts were consumed with worry for her brother, Liam. Her parents would never forgive her if anything happened to him in their absence. As the elder sibling, she was expected to be responsible and mature, yet she often felt she was neither.

They reached the lobby and approached the glass entry doors, but no car awaited them.

"Alright, Marco. Where's this driver?"

"He'll be here in a minute, Lucia. Look at the roads outside. Driving in that can't be easy." Marco gestured to the snow-covered street.

Peering through the glass, Lucia saw the street buried under a thick blanket of snow, untouched by plows. She crossed her arms and tapped her foot impatiently, eyes scanning for the car Marco had ordered.

Five minutes later, a large black SUV rolled up to the curb. Lucia glanced back at Marco. "Is that for us?"

"That's the one," he affirmed, opening the door and ushering her out.

"The limo wasn't available?" she asked, her voice tinged with annoyance.

"Not in weather like this," he replied, opening the back door for her.

Hiking up her dress, she climbed into the seat as Marco circled to the other side.

"Can you please take us to Children's Hospital?" she leaned forward and asked the driver. "As quickly as you can."

The driver nodded and set off down the snowy road. Lucia couldn't stop fidgeting, anxiety gnawing at her as they navigated the treacherous streets. She glanced at Marco, who appeared calm and collected, fully immersed in his phone.

"He's probably texting his wife another excuse for why he's not home yet," she thought bitterly.

Why he hadn't spent Christmas Eve at home with her was beyond her understanding. She hoped that her future husband would never pull a stunt like that when she would eventually marry.

The Children's Hospital was only eight blocks from the hotel, but the journey felt interminable.

"Can't you go any faster?" Lucia's voice pierced through the car, laced with mounting irritation.

"It's the roads, ma'am," the driver replied evenly. "If I increase the speed, we might slip."

She scoffed and slumped back into her seat. Finally putting his phone down, Marco turned to her and gently patted her knee. "I'm sure your brother will be alright."

"Do you know that for sure?" she snapped. Marco remained silent, wisely choosing not to respond. Lucia crossed her arms and gazed out the window, watching the snow fall thickly. It had been years since she'd seen a Christmas Eve blanketed in such a heavy snowfall.

Minutes later, they arrived at the hospital entrance. Marco and Lucia exited the SUV and hurried through the double doors. The reception area was festooned with red and green garlands, and a little dancing Santa figurine twirled merrily on the desk.

"Hello, can I help you?" The receptionist greeted them with a warm smile.

"Yes, I'm looking for my brother, Liam Romano," Lucia replied, her voice tight with anxiety.

"Okay, let's see." The receptionist began typing into her computer. As they waited, Lucia turned to Marco.

"Maybe you should wait down here in case my brother is awake and wonders who you are."

Marco smiled. "Sure, babe."

Turning back to the receptionist, Lucia's impatience grew. "Can't you just tell me his room number already?"

"Just one more moment, ma'am," the receptionist said sweetly. "The system is a little slow tonight because of the storm."

Lucia let out a heavy sigh and tapped her finger on the desk. She glanced at Marco, who had settled on a sofa in the waiting area, watching a Christmas cartoon on the TV.

"Alright, here we are. Your brother is in room 521. You can take the elevators around the corner and then left on the fifth floor–"

"I'm sure I'll find it," Lucia interrupted. She hurried to the elevators and pressed the button, her patience long exhausted by the slow car ride and the receptionist's leisurely pace. She needed to see her brother and assure herself that he was alright.

The elevator doors parted, and she stepped inside with a nervous urgency, repeatedly pressing the button for the fifth floor as if the fervor of her actions could hasten the ascent. Her heart raced in tandem with the ascending floor numbers. She darted out when the doors opened again, only to collide with a man traversing the corridor.

"Do you not have eyes?" she exclaimed, but he offered no response. Her breath caught in her throat as recognition dawned—it was the same man from the hotel who had collided with her and dropped his package earlier. Indeed, he must be blind to have stumbled into her twice in one night.

"Perhaps you should consider getting glasses," she called after him, yet he remained silent, his gaze unwavering from the path ahead. "So rude," Lucia muttered, watching his retreating form.

His posture caught her attention—head bowed low, shoulders slumped. He moved with the weariness of someone bearing a heavy burden. It was, after all, a hospital.

Glancing at the signs by the elevator, she noted that room 521 lay to the left. The man was heading in that direction, too. For a fleeting moment, she feared he might be entering her brother's room, but he disappeared into room 517, right beside it. She steeled herself, took a deep breath, and stepped into room 521, bracing for the possible sight of her brother ensnared in a web of medical machinery.

To her astonishment, she found him sitting upright, savoring a bowl of chocolate pudding. Relief washed over her as she approached him.

"Liam, what happened? Are you alright?" Her eyes roved over him, noting the bandage encasing his wrist and the Band-Aid on his forehead, but otherwise, he seemed unscathed.

"Yeah, I'm fine," he replied nonchalantly. "But you might need to talk to the cop when he comes back. He's the one that brought me here, and I don't think he's very happy with me."

She rolled her eyes. "Liam, what in God's Name happened?"

He shrugged. "I got bored, so…"

"And what happened to your wrist?" she interrupted, lifting his arm rather roughly.

"It's a sprain," a voice behind her answered. She turned to find a kind-looking man in a white coat and wire-rimmed glasses standing there.

"He and his friends thought it would be a good idea to climb onto the roof and come down the chimney like Santa Claus would. He was fortunate to land on a soft patch of snow. Otherwise, we might be dealing with something far more serious. Hello, I'm Dr. Wexler."

Lucia shook his hand. "Thank you, Doctor, for taking care of my brother. Our parents are out of town, and he seems to think he can do whatever he wants."

"Boys will be boys," the Doctor remarked with a bemused chuckle. "But he does have a slight bump on his head. I'd prefer to keep him overnight for observation, just to ensure there's no concussion."

Lucia nodded, her expression stern. "I Understand. It serves him right to spend the night in the hospital after acting so recklessly."

"Come on, Lucia. It wasn't that bad," Liam muttered, spooning more chocolate pudding into his mouth.

The Doctor excused himself, leaving the siblings alone. "I'll give you two some time."

Lucia turned her gaze to Liam, her frustration palpable. "Of all the foolish things you've done, Liam, this really takes the cake." She sank into a nearby chair just as a female officer carrying a cup of coffee entered the room.

"Hello, Miss Romano. I'm Officer Peterson. We spoke on the phone earlier?" She extended her free right hand.

Lucia stood and shook her hand. "Hi, Officer. Thank you for bringing my brother to the hospital. Is he going to be charged with anything? He may be a moron, but he is not a criminal."

Officer Peterson chuckled and took a sip of her coffee. "I'll have to agree with you there. Since there is no law against climbing onto your own roof, there won't be any charges. But don't let me catch you up there again, you hear me, young man?"

Liam nodded sheepishly. "I think my curiosity for roof climbing is satisfied."

"Alright then. It was nice meeting you, Lucia. Merry Christmas."

"Merry Christmas to you too, Officer," Lucia replied with a polite smile as she walked out.

"That was a lucky break," Liam said from behind her.

Lucia's smile faded as she turned to face him. "Yes, it was. And don't think Mom and Dad won't hear about this. They'll never leave you alone again."

"Oh, come on, Lucia! It's a little sprain."

"And possibly a concussion," she now more gently added. "Now get some rest. I'll be back in the morning to pick you up. We can spend Christmas morning together like we used to. How does that sound?"

Liam gave her a reluctant smile. "It sounds good, Sis. Thanks."

Lucia leaned over and kissed him on the forehead. "Alright. Good night."

"Good night." Liam settled back into his bed as Lucia pulled the covers over him and turned to leave the room. She couldn't take the guilt that gnawed at her—she should have been home with him instead of at a meaningless party with Marco. Liam always did dumb stuff, and even though he had convinced their parents he didn't need anyone to stay with him, she knew better. Tomorrow, she'd pack a bag and stay at the house with him until their parents got back.

As she stepped into the hall and walked towards the elevators, she noticed the door to Room 517 was ajar, a soft light spilling from within. Curiousness getting the better of her made her pause and peek inside.

The man she had seen earlier was sitting in a chair beside the hospital bed, his back to her. She approached the doorframe quietly, not wanting to disturb him.

He was holding the hand of a girl who looked to be in middle school, perhaps eleven or twelve. She appeared pale and frail, her small body connected to various machines, a breathing tube inserted into her mouth. The slow, steady beeping of the heart monitor filled the room as the man gently rubbed his thumb over her knuckles. The girl's eyes were closed, her chest rising and falling rhythmically—she was asleep.

Lucia had never seen a child look so ill. Her brother had been hospitalized with pneumonia when he was younger, but even then, he had not looked as fragile as this girl. She seemed to be on the brink of death. The man must be her father—there could be no other reason for him to be at the hospital so late on Christmas Eve, watching over his daughter as she slept.

♫CHAPTER SIX♫

An Epiphany

Lucia felt a profound stir within her as she observed the tender, intimate moment shared between father and daughter. The room was barren of any other presence, both inside and out, suggesting the absence of a mother. It was solely this man, exerting every effort for his ailing daughter, whose remaining time in this world seemed unguaranteed. Lucia chastised herself for her earlier behavior, for shouting at him after their accidental collision. It dawned on her that he had been too distraught to respond, particularly when the package he carried shattered upon impact.

The package he had been carrying was neatly wrapped in brown paper, reminiscent of a Christmas present. It must have been intended for his daughter, and after its content broke, he was left with nothing to give her. No wonder he appeared so despondent.

What could have been inside that box? She pondered. The fragments were pink and white, resembling glass, suggesting something feminine, fragile, and delicate. The sound it made as it fell was a heavy thud, implying a substantial object—perhaps a figurine or a vase of flowers. Stepping further into the room, her eyes roved over the walls adjacent to the hospital bed.

The decor made it clear that the girl had been hospitalized for some time. Drawings and posters adorned every inch of the wall, depicting roses, cats, and ballerinas, along with what seemed to be her own sketches of her father, her school, and various flowers and doodles. Ballet slippers hung next to a picture of the girl in a tutu and tiara, looking much healthier, standing beside her father, who beamed at the camera, holding a bouquet of flowers obviously meant for her. Evidently, this man was a devoted father, willing to do anything for his little girl.

The same Christmas movie Lucia had watched earlier at the hotel flickered on the TV, its sound muted. Another wave of emotion surged through her as she now remembered watching this movie with her parents at the same age as the girl. Perhaps this father and daughter shared the same tradition, so he had put it on for them to watch together.

As she leaned against the doorframe, gazing at one of her favorite scenes from the movie, her eyes caught sight of another drawing below the television. Stepping forward, she squinted to discern the details. The object in the drawing was pink and white, rectangular in shape. Atop a small platform stood a delicate ballerina, a circular mirror behind her attached to what appeared to be a lid. A music box, she realized. It resembled the one she cherished in her youth, the one her mother sold at a yard sale years ago, a loss that had left her heartbroken. The drawing revealed that this girl cherished her music box just as much.

As she surveyed the room, filled with the girl's belongings, the music box was nowhere to be found. Perhaps her father had left something so precious at home, safe from being knocked over or broken. Yet, wouldn't it make more sense to bring it here, to the hospital, to offer comfort? The room brimmed with mementos from her life; why not bring her the music box, too?

Her gaze returned to the drawing. "A pink and white music box... just like the shards of glass on the floor," she thought. Just before it hit the ground, the clunking sound from the package resembled that of a heavy glass box.

The realization struck her with a force that until that moment had been unknown to her. It all made sense now, Lucia thought. The music box had been in the package, and it had been smashed to smithereens when she had collided with him at the hotel. No wonder he looked so crushed. He must have been on his way to the hospital, bringing the music box as a gift for his daughter, and now he had nothing to give her.

She backed out of the room silently and sank onto a bench in the hallway, thinking she had played a significant role in ruining this family's Christmas. Lucia never thought of herself as a bad person, but at that moment, she felt like the worst human being on the planet. She had treated the man so poorly when he had done nothing wrong, all because she had been too self-absorbed and focused on having a good time with Marco.

She hung her head and let out a long sigh, feeling worse now than at the hotel. She had to do something, to find a way to right the wrong she had caused. If not for herself, then for the sick little girl lying just a few feet away from her. Pulling out her phone, she checked the time. It was 1:30 AM. It was late, but not too late. She still had time before it was truly Christmas morning.

Standing up, she walked to the elevator and pressed the down button. She knew now what she had to do. She would find a music box and return it to the man and his daughter before sunrise. She was determined to give the girl her Christmas present and wouldn't rest until she found it.

As the elevator doors parted with a hushed sigh, she stepped into the chamber and repeatedly pressed the button marked 'Lobby' with an almost frantic urgency. Her feet, aching from the cruel embrace of high heels worn throughout the evening, were a distant torment compared to the matter at hand.

When the elevator descended and the doors opened, she emerged and headed directly to the waiting area. There, sprawled upon the sofa like a fallen statue, lay Marco, ensnared in the depths of sleep. She seated beside him, her hand reaching out to rouse him from his slumber.

"Marco? Marco!" she called, her voice a mixture of tenderness and urgency.

"Wha—what? What is it?" He stirred, his hand rubbing the remnants of sleep from his eyes until his gaze focused on her. "Oh, hey. Is your brother alright?"

"He's fine, just a sprained wrist," she replied, her voice steady. "But there's something I need you to do for me."

A dreamy smile spread across his face. "What's that, sweet lips?"

Ignoring his saccharine endearment, she pressed on. "I need you to call your driver and get him back here. I have to run out to a store."

"Are you crazy? There's no store open right now. What do you need? We could just head back to the hotel and finish our night there, you know..." His fingers traced a languid path up her arm.

She shook her head resolutely. "Not yet, Marco. We can't go back to the hotel now. I need to go to a store. There must be at least one that's still open."

He stifled a yawn. "I don't think you're going to find one, darling. Even the ones with extended hours are closed by now. Are you trying to get me a last-minute Christmas gift?" He chuckled softly. "Because I can think of something you could give me that can't be bought in any store." His eyebrows danced suggestively.

Rolling her eyes, she stood, her resolve unshaken. "Can you just call your driver, please?"

"Alright, alright, I will." Marco pulled out his phone and began dialing.

Meanwhile, Lucia retrieved her own phone, her fingers deftly searching for stores open nearby. No options appeared, save for a single department store across town open throughout the night. It was her solitary hope. They had to have a music box resembling the one in the girl's drawing. Failure was not an option she was willing to entertain.

"The driver will be here in a few minutes. He's parked in the deck," Marco informed her, snapping his phone shut. "Now, will you tell me why you suddenly need to go shopping?"

"Do you remember when we first arrived at the hotel, and I bumped into that man coming off the elevator?"

Marco's eyes narrowed in thought. "Vaguely."

Lucia nodded, her expression earnest. "Yes, me too, at first. But when his package fell and broke, I didn't realize it then, but it turned out to be a Christmas gift for his daughter... a music box. I need to find a replacement, so he has something to give her on Christmas morning."

Marco regarded her as though she were truly mad. "Do you know that guy or something?"

She shook her head, her determination unwavering. "Never met him in my life. But I have to do this, Marco. And I won't rest until that music box is in his hands."

♫CHAPTER SEVEN♫

Elusive Redemption

As the driver maneuvered the vehicle to the front, Lucia and Marco emerged from the hospital's warmth into the snowy night, stepping into the awaiting SUV. The snow, though still falling, had lessened its earlier intensity, blanketing the streets in a serene whiteness.

"I need you to take me to this store," Lucia leaned forward, showing the driver her phone. "I know it's late, but they're still open."

The driver nodded, and they set off toward the department store. Lucia rested back into her seat, her eyes tracing the snow-laden streets as they drifted past.

"What if they don't have the music box?" Marco asked, his voice cutting through the quiet hum of the engine.

Lucia sighed, turning to face him. "Then we move on to the next store."

Marco ran a hand through his hair, frustration evident in his gesture. "Lucia, it's past midnight on Christmas Eve. Nothing's going to be open... I'm surprised this place hasn't closed already. They must be desperate."

"I have to hold on to hope, Marco. That man was just trying to bring his daughter a Christmas present, and I ruined it. I have to make it right. I can't just let it go—I'd feel terrible."

"You've never even met him?" Marco's eyebrows raised in disbelief.

Lucia shook her head. "I saw him at the hospital. I was visiting my brother and noticed the man entering the next room and sitting beside a very sick girl. I'm pretty sure she's his daughter. I saw a drawing of a pink and white music box that looked just like the shattered pieces I found near the elevator at the hotel. He must have been bringing it to her as a gift. Now, because of me, he has nothing to give. I have to find that music box, Marco, no matter what."

Marco chuckled softly. "I didn't know you had such a bleeding heart."

Lucia shrugged, a faint smile playing on her lips. "Just trying to do something nice. It is Christmas, after all."

Marco glanced down at his phone, nodding absentmindedly. "Yes, it is."

Lucia wondered if his thoughts had turned to his wife. She was probably still waiting, questioning his absence on Christmas Eve. What kind of husband spends Christmas Eve with another woman? The thought flitted through her mind, but she pushed it aside. Marco's philandering was the last thing she wanted to dwell on at that moment.

At long last, they arrived at the imposing department store, its red sign flashing ominously on the snowy night. Lucia stepped out of the SUV, Marco trailing close behind. Though she didn't necessarily need his assistance, she appreciated the extra set of eyes.

Inside, they meticulously combed through aisles and shelves, navigating the vast expanse of the store. It had everything imaginable except for the elusive music box. As they made their way back to the entrance, Lucia sighed heavily.

"Well, we'll have to find the next open store and look there. I'm not stopping until I find that box."

Marco stifled a yawn as he held the door open for her. "Alright, let's go find another store."

They drove around the city for over an hour, searching for any sign of an open shop or even one with workers inside they could convince to let them in. Each time, they came up empty-handed. It was now 3:00 AM, and both were tired and cold. Despite the exhaustion, Lucia's resolve remained unbroken. There had to be another way, she thought. Unless a miracle occurred, it seemed unlikely that she would find a music box before sunrise.

"So, where should we go next?" Marco asked. "Do you want to call it a night and go back to the hotel?"

Lucia leaned her head back, closing her eyes. "There's got to be someplace we haven't been yet." Turning to Marco, she asked, "Can you think of any place that might be open and have a music box?"

Marco stared out the window, deep in thought. "Hmm, let me think. You know, I have a friend, Joe, who might be able to help."

Lucia looked puzzled. "Your friend Joe can help us find what we're looking for in the middle of the night?"

Marco nodded. "Joe's a fireman, and he mostly works overnight shifts. He's always up around this time and probably at home since it's Christmas. But he lives out in the suburbs, so it may take us a while to get there."

"Well, if he can help, we should give it a chance," Lucia said, a glimmer of hope igniting within her.

♫CHAPTER EIGHT♫

A Difficult Request

Marco smiled and leaned forward to give the driver the address to Joe's house. The journey would take almost an hour, especially with the hazardous road conditions. As they set off, Lucia felt a renewed determination, silently praying that this lead would bring them the music box she desperately sought.

Lucia settled into her seat, listening to Christmas songs drifting softly from the radio. Her eyelids grew heavy, and as she felt herself succumbing to sleep, a recurring thought interrupted the feeling. She turned to Marco and gently shook his arm, rousing him from his slumber.

"What? What?" He blinked, disoriented.

"You never told me why you think your friend Joe can help with the music box."

Marco chuckled. "Oh, right. Well, I was talking to him a couple of weeks ago, and he mentioned he was going to buy a music box for his daughter. So I thought he might know where to find one, or maybe we could even buy it from him."

Lucia blinked in disbelief. "So, after I've been talking about this music box all night and dragging us all over town, you didn't think to mention this sooner?"

Marco shrugged. "You're right... it probably would have helped."

With that, Marco fell back asleep, leaving Lucia to her thoughts. The more time she spent with Marco outside their usual contexts, the more she realized he was somewhat dim. But, at least, they were heading towards someone who might have what she needed. She hoped Joe would be willing to part with it, and she could replace it once the stores reopened. She needed that music box tonight.

About fifty minutes later, the driver pulled into a quiet neighborhood, the houses adorned with twinkling lights and cheerful snowmen. They arrived at a modest home, its porch light still on. Lucia glanced at her phone; it was 3:52 AM.

Marco woke up as they parked, looking around. "Oh great, we're here."

"This friend, Joe...is he a good friend?" Lucia asked hesitantly. "I don't want to intrude on his home in the middle of the night."

"Joe and I go way back," Marco reassured her, patting her hand. "Don't worry. I texted him a while ago... he knows we're coming."

Marco climbed out of the SUV and helped Lucia out. The snow had stopped, but the temperature had dropped, making the driveway and sidewalk icy. Lucia regretted her choice of heels, longing for warmer, more practical footwear. After tonight, she vowed not to dress up until spring—thick, cozy turtlenecks and boots would be her go-to.

They approached the door, the cold biting at their exposed skin. Lucia took a deep breath, hoping Joe would be understanding and willing to help.

As they reached the door, Marco knocked softly, trying not to wake up the rest of Joe's household. A few moments later, the door creaked open.

"Marco! What a sight for sore eyes! Come on in."

As they stepped inside, Lucia was immediately enveloped in warmth. A gentle fire blazed in the fireplace, and a large Christmas tree adorned the corner of the living room, surrounded by a mountain of presents. It was a friendly, welcoming home, Lucia thought.

"And who have you brought with you?" Joe asked, grinning as he glanced at Lucia.

Marco made the introductions, and Lucia shook Joe's hand.

"I'm so sorry for barging in on you like this, Joe. You must think we're crazy," Lucia said apologetically.

Joe grinned. "It's fine. I'm not sure if Marco told you, but I'm a night owl. I just finished wrapping all the kids' presents and was about to have a cup of hot cocoa. Would you like to join me?"

Lucia sighed with relief. "That actually sounds wonderful, thank you."

They followed Joe into the kitchen, where he filled three mugs with hot chocolate and marshmallows. Lucia and Marco sat at the table, savoring the warmth of the drinks.

After taking her first sip, Lucia looked over at their host. "I'm sure you're wondering why we're here, Joe."

Sitting down to join them, Joe grinned and took a sip from his own mug. "I am a little curious."

Lucia took a deep breath. Joe was very kind, but she hardly knew him and wasn't sure how to begin.

"It's about the music box," Marco said bluntly.

"The music box?" Joe looked puzzled. "You mean the one I bought for my daughter?"

Lucia nodded. "You see, I need to find a music box to give to someone on Christmas morning, and it's very important that I find one tonight... or what's left of tonight. When Marco mentioned that you bought one, I thought you might be able to help me out. Could you sell it to me? Or at least let me borrow it, and I'll bring you a new one in the next few days?"

Joe leaned back, considering her request. "That's quite the request," he said slowly. "I understand how important this might be, especially on Christmas, and I really wished I could help... but..."

He got up and paced around the room as if weighing the pros and cons of parting with his daughter's much-desired gift. After a few moments, Joe sighed, sat back down, and gave Lucia a sympathetic look. "I'm sorry, but I just can't give it to you. My daughter has wanted this music box for a long time, and I don't want to disappoint her."

Lucia nodded, swallowing her disappointment. "I understand. I guess it never hurts to try, right?"

Joe took another sip from his mug. "I could probably find something else for you–"

Lucia held up her hand. "No, no. That won't be necessary. It's only a music box I'm looking for. I'm sorry we came all this way to disturb you."

Joe smiled warmly. "You didn't disturb me at all. Like I said, I was already up, and I always love a visit from Marco. We go way back."

As the two men began reminiscing, Lucia stood up. "Could you point me to the bathroom?"

"Sure, no problem. It's just down the hall, second door on the left."

Lucia left the kitchen and headed down the hall. As she passed by the living room, her eyes were drawn to the mountain of presents beneath the tree.

"It seems like Joe's daughter is going to receive much more than just a music box this year," she pondered. "Therefore, does she truly need the box? I doubt she will even miss it," Lucia murmured as she allowed her desperation to guide her actions.

♫CHAPTER NINE♫

A Child's Wisdom

Lucia crouched down, examining the colorfully wrapped boxes. Picking up each one, she gave them a gentle shake. When she lifted a rectangular box wrapped in pink paper, she immediately felt it was the music box. It made a distinctive clunking noise as she shook it lightly.

Not entirely sure what possessed her, she began to unwrap the present, tossing the wrapping paper behind her. Inside the white box, she found the exact music box she had seen in the girl's drawing at the hospital. It was glass, with pink and white stripes encircling it. As she lifted the lid, a small ballerina figurine began to twirl, accompanied by a sweet, delicate tune. She watched, mesmerized by the beauty of the box. When the song ended, she closed the lid and held the box, examining every detail. This had to be the exact one the man had dropped. There was no doubt.

She placed the music box back in its container and paused, staring at it. What was she doing? Was she really going to steal the music box from Joe and his daughter? She didn't want to do it, but she was desperate. This was the only way she could make things right for that man from the hotel and his sick daughter.

Her heart pounded as she weighed her options. She didn't want to betray Joe's kindness, but the thought of the little girl waking up without her gift gnawed at her conscience. Lucia took a deep breath and made up her mind. She would return the music box as soon as possible, but tonight, it had to go to someone who needed it even more.

"Merry Christmas! Are you Santa's helper?"

Lucia felt her heart stop. She turned towards the voice, slowly, music box in hand, to see a young boy no more than eight years old rubbing sleep from his eyes and smiling at her.

"H-hi, no, I'm not Santa's helper," Lucia managed a smile back. "What's your name?"

"Joshua," he replied. "What's yours?"

"My name is Lucia. A friend and I just came to visit your dad."

Joshua nodded. "Oh. What are you doing with my sister's Christmas present?"

Lucia looked down at the box in her hands and set it on the ground. "I was just taking a look," she told him, feeling awful for almost stealing a present under a Christmas tree, one meant for a child no less.

"Would you like some cookies? I know they were meant for Santa, but I don't think he would mind if you had one."

Lucia smiled warmly as the boy picked up a plate of sugar cookies from a table next to the tree and held it out to her. She took a cookie and bit into it. "Thank you, this is delicious."

Joshua grinned, revealing a missing front tooth. "My sister and I made them and decorated them ourselves."

"Well, you did a very good job," Lucia told him, putting the box back under the tree.

"Are you going to take my sister's present?" he asked, looking from her to the box.

Lucia sat down on the floor, her heart heavy with guilt. Being welcomed into this home in the middle of the night with open arms, only to almost steal a gift—it wasn't who she was.

"To tell you the truth, Joshua, I was going to take your sister's present," Lucia admitted. "But I can't do that, even though someone needs it very badly."

Joshua sat down next to her. "Who?"

Lucia smiled. "Yes, I can. There's a father who bought a music box for his daughter. His daughter is very sick, and she's in the hospital. The father wanted nothing more than to give her the music box on Christmas morning, and on his way to the hospital, I broke it by accident. Now I need to find a new one to give him, and I've searched every open store tonight and haven't found anything. All I want to do is make things right, and that's why I tried to take your sister's present. I am so sorry, and I hope you can forgive me."

Wise beyond his years, the boy put a hand over hers and smiled. "I think it is a good idea to replace the music box that was broken, and I know the girl will like it very much. I think it's okay for you to take the music box. I will give my sister one of my presents so you can have this one."

Joshua lifted the box and put it in her hands. Lucia's eyes began to water as Joshua stood up and wandered back down the hall to his bedroom.

"Hey Joshua," she tearfully called out as he reached for his bedroom door. "Merry Christmas!"

He smiled back at her with his gap-toothed grin. "Merry Christmas, Lucia."

She watched as he closed his bedroom door, then looked down at the present in her hands.

"He's right, you know. You should have it."

Lucia looked up to see Joe and Marco standing in the doorway to the living room.

"I'm so sorry, Joe. I don't know what came over me," she said. "And I'm sorry I kept your son up."

Joe shook his head. "Don't worry about it. After hearing your story, I can wholeheartedly agree with him. That little girl in the hospital deserves to have her music box, and my daughter will understand once I tell her."

She stood up, carefully holding the box. "I'm going to replace it and bring a new music box back to you as soon as the stores are open."

Joe chuckled. "That's alright, Lucia. Just knowing that it will make a sick little girl happy is payment enough."

Lucia walked over and hugged Joe with one arm, holding the box tightly with the other. She kissed him on the cheek and smiled. "You are a very generous man, Joe, and so is your son. I hope you have a very Merry Christmas."

"I hope you do, too, Lucia."

After Marco and Joe said their goodbyes, he and Lucia returned to the SUV. The driver had fallen asleep and woke up with a start when they opened the back doors.

"Sorry!" Lucia called up to him. "We're ready to go back to the hospital now."

The driver nodded, putting his hat back on. "Right away, ma'am."

She hugged the present to her chest, feeling triumphant and happy that they had finally found a music box to bring to the little girl. Lucia felt better than she had all night. She was finally getting the chance to right her wrong, all before the sun came up.

As they drove out of Joe's neighborhood and passed all the twinkling lights again, Lucia smiled. She couldn't wait to see the man's and his daughter's faces when she returned the music box to the hospital. Settling back in her seat, she stared out the window, watching as the night sky started to get lighter with the promise of dawn on the horizon. Christmas morning was almost here.

♫CHAPTER TEN♫

Matthew 19:14

It was nearly dawn by the time they returned to the city. Fortunately, the plow trucks had already cleared the roads. Lucia gazed out the window as they drove, watching the cityscape draped in a blanket of pristine snow. The sidewalks, benches, streetlamps, and the front steps of buildings were all adorned with a layer of white, resembling icing on a cake, she mused.

Leaning back in her seat, Lucia sighed deeply. A sense of renewal washed over her, filling the void that had plagued her the night before. The previous evening's misery and emptiness had dissipated, replaced by an unexpected surge of happiness and joy.

"What a waste of a night."

Frowning, Lucia glanced at Marco as he stirred, scratching the shadow of a beard on his face. "And what a waste of a hotel room."

"I'm sorry about the hotel room, but I don't think the night was a waste." Lucia turned to him. "I believe the night was spent doing something noble and kind."

He shrugged; his expression indifferent. "If you want to call it that, sure. I just think our time could've been better spent, especially in that hotel suite."

She rolled her eyes, exasperated. "Well, excuse me for wanting to do something nice for someone else on Christmas."

"But that's just it, Lucia. It's not in your nature to do good deeds and stay out all night on a wild goose chase for some stupid music box. When I met you, you were wild and carefree, loved parties, and didn't care what anyone thought. I admired your recklessness and your constant search for a good time. It was exactly what I wanted in a casual relationship. But now... now

I'm not so sure. I think maybe our priorities aren't really aligned anymore."

At that moment, they pulled up to the hospital. Lucia looked at the double sliding doors at the entrance, recognizing the same cheerful receptionist inside. "I think maybe you're right, Marco."

"I am? About which part?" he asked, his tone cautious.

"Our priorities don't align, Marco. Maybe I don't want to be the wild and crazy girl anymore, and if that's what you need, then you should probably look elsewhere. I feel a miserable emptiness inside whenever I act selfishly. Maybe I'm finally learning I have a conscience. And I know I don't want a meaningless relationship with you anymore."

He let out a derisive snort. "So, it's over?"

"Yes, Marco, it's over. We're wrong for each other, especially outside the bedroom. And by the way, I found your wedding ring last night when it fell out of your jacket pocket. Does your wife know you've been cheating on her?"

Marco's face turned ashen. "I didn't want you to know about her."

Lucia frowned, her eyes hardening. "You should've told me you were married. Who knows if I would've gone through with it if I did, but I know now that the last thing I want is to be involved with a married man. And I can't believe you're not with her on Christmas."

Marco stayed silent, a shadow of guilt crossing his features as Lucia continued.

"I don't want to be 'the other woman' anymore. You should go home to your wife or, better yet, tell her the truth. She deserves that, at the very least."

"Maybe you're right," Marco said softly.

Lucia turned to him, surprised to hear the words come out of his mouth. "I am?"

"My wife and I have been unhappy for years. I just wanted to add some fun and excitement to my life, and that's why I was so attracted to you. You were carefree and had zero baggage, and I thought that was the perfect solution. But I can see now that you're right. I need to come clean with my wife about the affairs."

"Affairs?!" Lucia exclaimed. "I wasn't the only one?"

Marco shook his head. "Not that many, but more than a few."

Lucia closed her eyes, a wave of revulsion washing over her. How had she ever been attracted to Marco? Now that he was showing his true colors, she realized how much of a slimeball he truly was.

"Well, goodbye, Marco. I hope you do better in life." Holding the box tightly, she opened the door and stepped out. Marco also opened his door and walked over to her side.

"Goodbye, Lucia. And don't worry about returning the clothes—they're yours to keep."

"Thanks, but I'll probably give this dress away," she told him.

He shrugged. "That's fine. Well, shall we part amicably?" He held out his hand.

Holding back a sigh, she took his hand and shook it.

"It was fun while it lasted," Marco said with a wink.

"Mmmhmm." She nodded, dropped his hand, and turned to go through the sliding double doors. She knew Marco was probably watching her as she walked inside, but she didn't look back even once.

"Well, hello and welcome back!" The receptionist greeted Lucia with a warm smile as she approached.

"Hello, and Merry Christmas," Lucia replied, her smile brightening. "I hope your shift ends soon so you can get some rest. You've been here all night."

The receptionist beamed. "That's very thoughtful of you, but don't worry. I'll be leaving shortly to spend Christmas morning with my family."

"That sounds lovely." Lucia adjusted the box in her arms. "Well, I have to get going."

"Merry Christmas to you, dear!" the receptionist called as Lucia walked toward the elevators.

She could hardly wait as she pressed the up button and watched the doors slide open. The music box felt heavy in her arms, but soon she would be relieved of it. Imagining the look on the man and his daughter's faces when she delivered it brought a smile to her lips. He would probably be completely shocked to see her, or maybe he wouldn't even recognize her. She looked forward to telling him the entire story of her quest to retrieve the music box.

And after that, she could check on her brother. Liam would probably be ready to go home after spending the night in the hospital. Maybe she could even introduce her brother to the man and his daughter since they had been neighbors through the night.

The elevator doors dinged open, and she stepped inside, pressing the button for the fifth floor. Room 517...she had memorized the number. She hoped they hadn't been moved, but given the personal effects in 517, she suspected it was likely the daughter's permanent residence.

As she anxiously tapped her foot, watching the numbers climb, butterflies fluttered in her stomach. This was her first time doing something so selfless for a stranger, and she hoped he wouldn't think she was some random intruder. No, that wouldn't happen, she reassured herself. Everything was going to go perfectly.

Finally, the doors opened, and she stepped onto the fifth floor. The corridor was adorned with red and green streamers, and a small Christmas tree stood beside the nurses' station, surrounded by tiny presents. She hurried down the hall with a broad smile, passing rooms 507, 509, 511... She was three doors away when a strange feeling crept over her. She slowed her pace, glancing around but seeing no one. Patients in rooms 513 and 515 sat on their beds, exchanging gifts with their parents. Lucia smiled as she passed by, but as she neared Room 517, a sense of unease settled in.

There was no sound coming from the room—no Christmas music, no cartoons on the TV. Holding her breath, she approached the door and peered inside. The man was seated in the same chair from the night before, his back to the door. The TV played an encore presentation of last night's movie, the sound muted, but it didn't matter; the man wasn't watching.

Unsure of what to do, she stood motionless for a full minute, observing him. He was still wearing the same clothes from the previous night, clearly having not left or even moved from that chair.

The girl lay still and quiet in the bed, apparently sleeping, as the man watched over her. Lucia didn't want to interrupt the peaceful moment, but if the girl was sleeping, she could at least get the man's attention and hand over the box. Then she could visit her brother and give them some privacy. Maybe later, when the girl woke up, she could come back to talk.

As she stepped slowly into the room, she noticed his shoulders were shaking. His head hung low as he wiped a tear from his face. He was crying, she realized, and had been for some time. She assumed that celebrating a joyous holiday like Christmas in a hospital must be hard, attributing his tears to the circumstances. Still, an uneasy feeling persisted as she took another step forward.

He held his daughter's hand, rubbing his thumb over her knuckles as he had done the night before. But there was a difference in his grip now—desperation perhaps as if he wasn't ready to let her go.

Suddenly, his shoulders stopped shaking, and he leaned back in his chair, rubbing a hand over his face. He looked exhausted, likely having stayed awake all night, she thought.

She clutched the box tightly to her chest, wanting to do something more for him. Of course, she had the music box, but she wished there was something more she could offer. Maybe she could sit by his daughter while he got some much-needed sleep or fetch him a cup of coffee or some breakfast. She wasn't sure what, but he needed something.

Glancing at the drawings on the wall, she smiled as she studied them again, starting with the music box and moving to the drawings of roses next to the bed. She would bring roses for the girl the next time she visited, hoping that the man would allow for a next time.

As Lucia started to clear her throat, she saw the man's head fall to the side. In his fatigue, he had fallen asleep. She turned to leave, deciding to return later, but was called back by a sudden movement that caught her attention. In his exhaustion, the man had dropped his daughter's hand. It hung lifelessly off the side of the bed.

Lucia's breath was trapped in her throat as she realized why the room was so quiet. All the machines monitoring the girl had been turned off—even the one helping her breathe. She now noticed that the breathing tube had been removed from her mouth as well.

Victor's daughter passed away not long before Lucia arrived. She was too late. She had stayed up all night and traversed the city to do something kind, but now it was too late. A tear slid down Lucia's face as she looked down at the box in her hands.

It had been so important for her to right the wrongs of the night before. She had wanted to bring a glimpse of joy into this girl's life. But now, that could never happen. The girl would never know Lucia or what she had done for her. She would never see the beautiful music box.

Lucia felt her arms grow heavy as they fell to her sides, and in that moment, the box slipped from her grasp, tumbling to the ground. It clunked heavily as it hit the floor, the lid springing open. As the delicate pink and white music box slipped from its place, it tumbled through the air and onto the floor, its shattering filling the room with an echo. The dainty music box was now a hundred tiny, sparkling fragments gleaming in the low light as they scattered across the floor.

♫THE END♫

ROBERTO JIMENEZ

Matthew 19:14

"Jesus said, 'Let the little children come to me, and do not hinder them, for the kingdom of heaven belongs to such as these.'"

About the Author

Roberto Jimenez is a dedicated educator, seasoned entrepreneur, and passionate storyteller. With over 15 years of experience in healthcare consulting, management, and quality assurance, Roberto brings a wealth of real-world insight to his writing. He holds degrees in nursing and business administration.

Currently, Roberto teaches high school science, health, and business in Miami, FL, where he inspires young minds to explore the intersections of science, health, and entrepreneurship. His journey from a robust career in healthcare to the dynamic world of education reflects his commitment to nurturing the next generation of leaders.

In addition to his professional pursuits, Roberto is deeply committed to his family. He enjoys spending quality time with his wife and three children, exploring new places, and engaging in creative activities such as photography, cooking, and writing together.

"The Music Box" is a labor of love, born from Roberto's observations during his university years and his desire to inspire empathy and awareness in others. Through his storytelling, he aims to remind readers of the profound impact their actions can have on the lives of those around them. Roberto's unique blend of professional expertise and personal experiences enriches his writing, offering readers a compelling and heartfelt narrative. He hopes "The Music Box" will touch your heart and encourage you to cherish the small moments and connections that define our humanity.

Also by the Author

About the Publisher

Learn more at https://uriartepublishing.com